D THE CONSTRUCTION CREW

Trucks on Vacation

Jodie Parachini

illustrated by
John Joven

Albert Whitman & Company
Chicago, Illinois

One warm summer morning,
the trucks were all snappy.
As temperatures rose,
they grew less and less happy.

When trucks get hot-tempered,
their moods are the worst.
If the trucks get too heated,
their gaskets might burst!

"There's tasks to be finished,
and work to be done.
But no one," said Digby,
"is finding it fun!"

"I've used all my coolant,"
said Lori the mixer.
Her engine had seized up,
and nothing could fix her.

“I’m melting,” cried Morris,
“and my treads feel like tar.
I can’t race around
like a zippy sports car!”

"You're going too slowly.
Can't you move any quicker?"
The trucks raised their axles
and started to bicker.

"It's Mack's fault," yelled Gaby.
"He's blocking the road."
"But Bruno and Juno
keep dropping their load!"

"TIME OUT!"

called the foreman,
who'd seen quite enough.
"More muscle, less tussle,
or I'm gonna get rough!"

With sweat on their bumpers
and grilles overheated,
the trucks felt their engines
and spirits depleted.

The heat made them dozy,
and sluggish and slow.
"What we need is a break,"
grumbled Mack, the backhoe.

Then Digby cried,

"YES!

We should act like a team,
to think up a method
for letting off steam."

He shifted his bucket
and whirled into gear.
"We can't go to the sea,
so let's...

BRING THE BEACH HERE!"

“Hooray!” cried the trucks.

“Our construction can wait.”
As they rushed to find tools
they could use to create...

“The Diggers’ Resort!
Comes complete with a lake.

The perfect relief for when
trucks need a break!”

The dumpers transported
a soft, sandy mountain.

While tanker trucks squirted
a fresh, cooling fountain.

Then Mack brought the beachballs,
and Morris the raft,

while Digby's new outfit
made everyone laugh.

But something was needed—
to deal with the heat—

then a jingle was heard
coming from the next street.

And when it arrived—
did it come from a dream?
The best truck of them all,
the one selling...

ICE CREAM!

The trucks are all chilling,
but Lori is reeling—her spark plugs ignited,
and so have her feelings!

The trucks take it easy,
relax, and unwind,

but tomorrow will come, and
it’s back to the grind!

Vacation is thrilling
but never lasts long,
so Digby and friends
end their day with a song.

Mix it! Grind it!
Lift and haul.

We're mighty trucks. We do it all!

Come on, gang.
Let's join the crew.

Today we're
building
something new!

For Nancy, Jan, and cousin Leo, who live in paradise—JP

To my wife, Ana. Thank you for letting me build this amazing life with you.—JJ

Library of Congress Cataloging-in-Publication data
is on file with the publisher.

Illustrations by John Joven
First published in the United States of America in 2023 by Albert Whitman & Company
ISBN 978-0-8075-1591-4 (hardcover)
ISBN 978-0-8075-1592-1 (ebook)

Printed in China
10 9 8 7 6 5 4 3 2 1 WKT 26 25 24 23 22

Design by Erin McMahon

For more information about Albert Whitman & Company,
visit our website at www.albertwhitman.com.